The Elephant in the Sukkah

For our precious grandsons, Ori and Yehuda
S. M.

KAR-BEN PUBLISHING, INC.
A division of Lerner Publishing Group, Inc.
241 First Avenue North
Minneapolis, MN 55401 USA
1-800-4-KARBEN

Website address: www.karben.com

Main body text set in Mikado bold
Typeface provided by HVD Fonts

Library of Congress Cataloging-in-Publication Data

Names: Mandell, Sherri Lederman, author. | Kuman, Ivana G., 1970– illustrator.
Title: The elephant in the sukkah / by Sherri Mandell ; illustrated by Ivana Kuman.
Description: Minneapolis : Kar-Ben Publishing, [2019] | Summary: Former circus
    elephant Henry follows the sound of music to the Broner family's sukkah and a little
    boy has a clever way to include Henry in the holiday fun.
Identifiers: LCCN 2018032670| ISBN 9781541522121 (lb : alk. paper) |
    ISBN 9781541522138 (pb : alk. paper)
Subjects: | CYAC: Elephants—Fiction. | Sukkah—Fiction. | Singing—Fiction. |
    Jews—Fiction.
Classification: LCC PZ7.1.M36455 El 2019 | DDC [E]—dc23

LC record available at https://lccn.loc.gov/2018032670

Manufactured in the United States of America
1-44397-34658-11/29/2018

The Elephant in the Sukkah

Sherri Mandell

illustrated by **Ivana Kuman**

KAR-BEN
PUBLISHING

Henry the elephant sang in the circus. He was a star.
Audiences from all over the world applauded him.

Years passed. Henry still loved to sing, but his voice had grown tired.

One day a new singer took the stage.

Henry was sent to a farm for old elephants.
Nobody there sang.
They slept. They munched on straw.
They complained about their aching trunks.

Poor Henry sang at dinner, but nobody joined him.

He sang in his bath, but nobody clapped.

He sang before he went to sleep, but everybody **shushed** him.

He sang in his bath, but nobody clapped.

He sang before he went to sleep, but
everybody **shushed** him.

He felt useless and lonely.
If only he had somebody to sing with.

And then one night he heard singing and music.
He put on his hat and walked away from the
elephant farm.

He approached a little hut next to a house.
The Brenners' Sukkah said a sign.

What's a sukkah? Henry thought.

And then he saw a family inside the hut.

There were many children and a dog and a cat.

They sang and played their instruments—song after song.

Henry longed to sing with them, but he didn't know any of the words.

The Brenners were so busy singing they didn't notice him.
So Henry listened quietly until he knew the words.

Then he went back to the elephant farm,
humming the songs he had learned.

The next night Henry heard the singing again.
He walked back to the Brenners' sukkah, and this time he sang along.

A little boy named Ori heard him singing and came outside.
"I didn't know elephants could sing!" said Ori.
Henry smiled at Ori. Ori smiled at Henry.

The following night Henry returned.
Ori brought the whole family to meet Henry.
"Come join us in our sukkah," Ori said.
"What is a sukkah?" asked Henry.

"It's a special kind of place where we live for a week during the holiday of Sukkot. We eat our meals in the sukkah and sometimes we even sleep in the sukkah," said Ori's mother.

"A sukkah must have at least three walls. And we have to be able to see the stars through the roof," said Ori's father.

"We sing in the sukkah too," added Ori.

"I would love to come into the sukkah and sing with you!" said Henry.

THE BRENNERS' SUKKAH

But there was no room in the sukkah for an elephant.

He stuck his trunk in.

He backed in.

He padded
sideways.

But Henry could not fit
through the door.

"This is the last night of the holiday," said Ori.
"We have to find a way to get you into the sukkah."
Ori looked up at the roof.
He looked around at the walls.
"I've got an idea," Ori said.

Ori whispered with his mom and dad. Together, they carefully removed one wall of the sukkah.

"You can be one wall of our sukkah!" said Ori.

"I'm happy to have such an important job," said Henry, delighted.

"Does it hurt to have the palm roof resting on your back?" asked Ori.

"Not at all," said Henry. "I'm getting a nice head scratch."

That night, Henry ate with the Brenners.
He laughed with them and sang with them.
Now Henry knew what a sukkah was:
a place to be together.
"Next year, I am going to build a sukkah and
invite you," said Henry.

And so he did.
There was plenty of room for everybody.
And when Henry and the Brenner family
sang, all the elephants hummed along.

THE BRENNERS' SUKKAH

Sukkot is a joyous holiday that lasts for seven days. It is a celebration of the fall harvest. Also known as the Festival of Booths, Sukkot recalls the temporary huts the Jewish people built and lived in as they wandered in the desert after the biblical Exodus from Egypt. It is traditional to eat and even sleep in the sukkah. A sukkah roof may be made of natural materials like tree branches or cornstalks. Sukkah walls may be built out of anything. The Talmud even states that one may use an elephant as a sukkah wall!

Sherri Mandell's books include the National Jewish Book Award winner, *The Blessing of a Broken Heart*. She is also the author of *Writers of the Holocaust* (Facts on File) and has been a contributor to USA Today, The Times of Israel, Hadassah Magazine, and The Jerusalem Post. *The Elephant in the Sukkah* is her first book for children. She lives in Israel.

Award-winning illustrator **Ivana Kuman** is a graduate of the Arts Academy in Zagreb. She has written and illustrated many picture books for children and is the author of 35 short animated children's films. She lives in Zagreb with her husband, two daughters, and a cat.